Dear Parents:

Congratulations! Your child is taking the first steps on an exciting journey. The destination? Independent reading!

STEP INTO READING® will help your child get there. The program offers five steps to reading success. Each step includes fun stories and colorful art or photographs. In addition to original fiction and books with favorite characters, there are Step into Reading Non-Fiction Readers, Phonics Readers and Boxed Sets, Sticker Readers, and Comic Readers—a complete literacy program with something to interest every child.

Learning to Read, Step by Step!

Ready to Read   Preschool–Kindergarten
• big type and easy words • rhyme and rhythm • picture clues
For children who know the alphabet and are eager to begin reading.

Reading with Help   Preschool–Grade 1
• basic vocabulary • short sentences • simple stories
For children who recognize familiar words and sound out new words with help.

Reading on Your Own   Grades 1–3
• engaging characters • easy-to-follow plots • popular topics
For children who are ready to read on their own.

Reading Paragraphs   Grades 2–3
• challenging vocabulary • short paragraphs • exciting stories
For newly independent readers who read simple sentences with confidence.

Ready for Chapters   Grades 2–4
• chapters • longer paragraphs • full-color art
For children who want to take the plunge into chapter books but still like colorful pictures.

STEP INTO READING® is designed to give every child a successful reading experience. The grade levels are only guides; children will progress through the steps at their own speed, developing confidence in their reading.

Remember, a lifetime love of reading starts with a single step!

Visit us on the Web!
StepIntoReading.com
rhcbooks.com

Educators and librarians, for a variety of teaching tools, visit us at RHTeachersLibrarians.com
ISBN 978-0-593-43136-8 (trade) — ISBN 978-0-593-43137-5 (lib. bdg.)
ISBN 978-0-593-43138-2 (ebook)

Printed in the United States of America
10 9 8 7 6 5 4 3 2

2022 Random House Children's Books Edition

STEP INTO READING®

STEP 3 · READING ON YOUR OWN

THE KINDNESS CLUB

by B.B. Arthur

Random House New York

All the outrageous members
of the L.O.L. Surprise! squad
are friends.
Some friends are into fashion.
Some friends are into fame.
But all these friends agree
that the best friends are kind.

MISS PUNK

©MGA

©MGA

©MGA

SHARING IS KIND

Surfer Babe shares her surfboard
with Splash Queen.

She knows how much
her friend loves the waves.
The beach is always more fab
when you share it with someone.

TAKING TURNS IS KIND

MC Swag and Honey Bun
take turns on the mic.

They pick out beats
for each other.
They love to hear
each other's rhymes.

INCLUDING OTHERS IS KIND

Dance Bot invites everyone to the dance floor.

10

©MGA

More dancers mean
more dancing!

Dance Bot knows
dancing is the most
fun with a crowd.

11

LISTENING IS KIND

Cosmic Queen wants to know
her friends' wildest dreams.

Soul Babe always listens
to her friends' deepest secrets.

©MGA

Listening helps them learn
about each other.

HELPING IS KIND

Sometimes Instagold needs help getting connected! She wants to share her latest pic online.

VRQT is a tech whiz.

She helps Instagold in a snap.

SAYING NICE THINGS IS KIND

"You rock!" says Boss Queen.

"You rule!" says Rocker.

BEING PATIENT IS KIND

Drag Racer loves to go fast.

©MGA

Flower Child likes to stop
and smell the flowers.

It may take a
little longer,
but a friend is
worth the wait.

ACCEPTING OTHERS IS KIND

It Baby likes to be fancy.

Grunge Grrrl likes to be casual.

Queen Bee loves
her curly, puffy hair.
Cosmic Queen loves her
rolls and curls.

They all tell
each other,
"I love your style!"

CHEERING FOR EACH OTHER IS KIND

When Supa Star is onstage, her voice is powerful. Hoops MVP cheers for her friend.

TEAM

#1 FAN

©MGA

When Hoops MVP is on the court,
her moves are flawless.
Supa Star cheers for her friend
just as loudly in return.

WORKING TOGETHER IS KIND

Miss Baby loves pageants.

Miss Punk loves punk rock.

©MGA

No matter how
different they are,
they agree that
they love the stage.

©MGA

KINDNESS FEELS GREAT!

Bon Bon feels extra sweet
when she is kind.

Neon QT feels extra bright

when someone is kind to her.

FRIENDS ARE KIND

Queen Bee is thankful
to have her squad around
her every day.

©MGA

She feels lucky to have such kind friends.

©MGA

©MGA

The L.O.L. Surprise! squad
love their clubs.
They have the glam club,
the glee club, and many more.
But in the end,
they are all in the same club—

the kindness club!

LET'S BE KIND

©MGA